SEA KEEPERS

Sea Otter Summer Camp

Coral Ripley

Special thanks to Sarah Hawkins
For Huxley Didymus-True

ORCHARD BOOKS

First published in Great Britain in 2021 by The Watts Publishing Group

1 3 5 7 9 10 8 6 4 2

Text copyright © Orchard Books, 2021
Illustrations copyright © Orchard Books, 2021

The moral rights of the author and illustrator have been asserted.

A CIP catalogue record for this book
is available from the British Library.

ISBN 978 1 40836 364 5

Printed and bound in Great Britain by Clays Ltd, Elcograf S.p.A.

The paper and board used in this book are made from wood from responsible sources.

Orchard Books
An imprint of
Hachette Children's Group
Part of The Watts Publishing Group Limited
Carmelite House
50 Victoria Embankment
London EC4Y 0DZ

An Hachette UK Company
www.hachette.co.uk
www.hachettechildrens.co.uk

 # Contents

Chapter One

Grace tapped her paddle on the side of
her bright red kayak impatiently. The
sky was blue with fluffy white clouds,
and the sea looked cool and inviting.
But Grace's kayak wasn't on the water
– it was still on the beach! She and her
friends, Emily and Layla, were all sitting
in kayaks on the sand while Pranav,
their instructor, walked around them,

teaching them how to paddle.

Grace sighed. She knew she had to learn how to use the little boat safely – her grandad was a fisherman and had always told her to respect the sea. But she couldn't wait to get into the water!

"We'll be off soon," Layla said with a grin. "Emily and I just need a bit more practice!"

Grace glanced over at Emily, who was struggling with her paddle. As she watched, Emily dug her paddle into the ground and flicked sand all over Pranav.

"Oops!" Emily gasped as Pranav coughed, shaking the sand out of his hair. "I'm so sorry!"

"Don't worry," he spluttered.

Emily tried again, and this time she got it right.

"OK, time to go in," announced Pranav.

"Yay!" cried Grace.

The girls jumped out and dragged their kayaks towards the waves.

"I hope it's easier on the water!" Emily said nervously.

"We'll help each other," Grace promised. "Come on!"

She pulled her kayak into the waves and Pranav held it still as she jumped in. He checked her life jacket and pulled the kayak's rubber skirt over her legs so they were tucked inside.

"This is actually really fun!" Emily exclaimed as they set off, paddling into the bay. The waves rocked their kayaks gently as they steered around the boats moored in the harbour.

"Yeah, it's better now I can't get a mouth full of sand," Pranav joked,

splashing at her with his paddle.

"I thought you liked *sand*wiches!" Layla joked.

Emily and Pranav groaned, but Grace grinned. It was a beautiful afternoon and she was out on the sea with her best friends. Even Layla's bad jokes were funny! She paddled as fast as she could and sped ahead, the kayak moving easily with each of her twists and turns. "I'm going to go round Grandpa's boat!" she called, paddling up to the fishing boat. She'd never seen The Salty Seahorse from this angle before! It was funny being so low down on the water. She felt like a duck floating on the surface.

As she paddled back to her friends, Grace noticed a strange shimmering rainbow patch on the water.

"Look!" she called out to the others. "It's the same colour as Marina's hair!"

Layla gasped dramatically. "Do you think it could be" – she dropped her voice to a whisper so that Pranav couldn't hear – "mermaid magic?"

The girls grinned at each other in excitement. They had a very special secret; they could magically turn into mermaids! It had started when they'd rescued a dolphin who was a mermaid's pet – and not just any mermaid, but a mermaid princess! Marina was the

princess of Atlantis, a mermaid kingdom hidden from human eyes by powerful magic. But when she had taken them to Atlantis, something even more amazing had happened – Grace, Emily and Layla had been chosen to be the Sea Keepers, whose job it was to find the Golden Pearls and stop an evil siren called Effluvia.

"I don't think it's magic," Emily said. "Besides, if Marina needed us, she'd send for us." She held up her wrist and her purple seashell bracelet sparkled in the sunlight.

Grace glanced down at her matching bracelet. Every time the Mystic Clam

remembered where another pearl
was hidden, Marina made their shell
bracelets glow. Grace wished they would
glow now!

"There's another one over there," Layla
said, pointing her paddle at another

rainbow-coloured patch. The girls kayaked over to look.

"Don't go any further than the buoys," Pranav called, pointing at the line of floating balls that marked the deeper water. "The open sea can be very dangerous."

"Especially with Effluvia around," Emily said with a shudder.

Grace frowned as she thought of the horrible siren. Sirens were a type of mermaid, but they used their magic for bad instead of good. They could control sea creatures and get them to do whatever they wanted. Effluvia had almost hypnotised them with her magic

15

once, but luckily Marina had broken the spell just in time!

The girls paddled around the harbour a few more times.

"I think that's enough for today," Pranav called.

"Aw! I'm finally getting the hang of this," said Emily.

The sun was beginning to set and the sky was being painted in pretty pinks and golden oranges. They paddled back towards the shore and Grace spotted an even bigger rainbow patch around a motorboat called Starfish.

"We'll have to ask Marina what that stuff is the next time we see her," Emily

said, peering at the colourful water curiously.

Grace felt chilly as they jumped into the water and splashed back to shore, pulling the kayaks behind them. Her arms had goosebumps on them.

Pranav opened a shed and started putting the kayaks away on tall racks. Grace helped Layla carry hers to the shed then she ran back to help Emily. "Thanks," Pranav said as Grace and Emily brought the kayak over. But as Grace passed him the paddles she noticed something – her bracelet was glowing!

She looked over at her friends, who were staring at their own bracelets.

17

"Thanks, Pranav. See you next week!" Grace said in a rush.

The three girls raced out on to the sand and went round to the back of the boatshed. No time would pass while they were having a mermaid adventure, but they didn't want anyone to see them magically disappear!

They held hands and chanted the magic words:

"Take me to the ocean blue,
Sea Keepers to the rescue!"

Grace grinned as a kaleidoscope of colours swirled around them. They were turning into mermaids!

18

Chapter Two

Grace flipped her fins and shot to the surface in a whoosh of bubbles. She was a mermaid again! She grinned as she looked down at her pink tail with its tiny scales and broad golden fins. If she had her mermaid tail at swim meets, she'd be sure to win every race!

"Grace!" Emily called.

Without losing speed, Grace did a flip

in the water and sped back down to her friends. Emily's tail was golden yellow and Layla's was aquamarine, but they both had pink fins that matched Grace's tail. They were next to another mermaid who had a lilac-coloured tail, purple-and-pink hair and a beautiful shell crown.

"Hi, Marina!" Grace said, grinning.

Princess Marina swam over to give her a hug. "I was just telling the others that we're in the Pacific Ocean! And I have something cool to show you . . ."

She dived down through the water and the girls followed eagerly. All around them were huge seaweeds towering from

the sea bed like trees in a rainforest. Marina took them down very deep, where it was dark and chilly. Grace felt goosebumps forming on her arms again.

"What are those?" Layla asked, pointing to some little spiny balls gathered at the bottom of the kelp trees.

"Sea urchins!" Marina said. "They move slowly but they can eat a lot of kelp."

"Those are animals?" Layla asked, staring at the spiky balls in amazement.

Grace had never seen one before, but she remembered her grandpa telling her about them. "Aren't they poisonous? People stand on them and get hurt."

Marina nodded. "They aren't poisonous to mermaids, but you still don't want to get spiked! But what I wanted to show you was this – look!" Marina pointed at a deep crack in the ground.

"Um, a . . . crack?" Emily said, confused.

"This is a gap between two tectonic plates," Marina explained. "There are seven enormous plates underneath the earth and the sea. Where they meet there are cracks like this one, caused by volcanoes and earthquakes."

"Oh, I thought we were going to see an amazing sea creature," Emily said, looking disappointed.

"Or some treasure," Layla exclaimed. "Do you remember when we found that pirate treasure? It was so shiny!"

"Maybe there *is* some treasure," Grace said excitedly. "Has the Mystic Clam remembered there's a pearl hidden here?"

"I think so," Marina said, nodding. "He gave me this riddle:

Stuck between two plates deep down in the ground,

Something must be broken for the pearl to be found."

Grace swam down and peered into the crack. It was even darker down there, and it looked like there were things scuttling about in the black water. She

thought it was a bit spooky!

Grace felt something touch her arm and she jumped in alarm, then felt a bit silly when she realised it was just a bit of slimy kelp brushing against her as it swayed in the tide. But then a shadow fell over her.

"Effluvia!" she shouted, her heart beating fast as she spun around in alarm.

"It's not Effluvia!" Emily reassured her. "It's just a sea otter."

They looked at the little creature with its sleek brown fur and friendly face. It galloped through the water, doing a sort of doggy paddle as it swam along.

"Hello!" Layla called.

"Have you seen a
pearl anywhere?"
Marina asked.
The otter
waved a clawed
foot, her whiskers
twitching as
bubbles came from
her mouth, then she
pointed up at the surface.

"I think she wants us to follow her!"
Layla said.

The girls grinned and flipped their
fins, chasing the otter up to the surface.
The water got warmer as they went up
through the kelp, until finally they burst

through the surface.

As Grace put her head above water she saw a grey, cloudy sky and heard lots of cheers and shouts.

"That was your best dive yet, Lola!" one voice called.

"How deep did you go?" asked another.

Grace blinked and brushed the water from her eyes. There were three other sea otters crowding around Lola.

"Almost to the bottom," Lola said proudly. She turned to the girls and grinned. "Sorry I startled you down there. I couldn't talk because I was almost out of breath!"

"That's OK!" Grace laughed.

27

"I'm Lola," the otter introduced herself. "And this is Adi, Rae and Maya!"

The otters waved as Lola said their names. Rae was the smallest, Maya had a white speckle on her nose and Adi was the biggest.

"I'm Marina, and these are the Sea Keepers – Emily, Grace and Layla." Marina quickly introduced them.

The young otters swam around them excitedly, hardly staying still for a second. Animal-mad Emily looked like she was in heaven, surrounded by otters! Then, to the girls' delight, the sea otters turned on their backs and held paws, so they were floating along together.

"Sea otters hold paws so they stay
together as a group," Marina whispered.
"It's called a 'raft'."

"That is the cutest thing I've ever
seen!" Emily squealed.

29

"I was practising for our diving competition," Lola told them. "We're having it later. You should come! I'll ask Kishi if you can stay. Kishi!"

Before the girls could say anything, the otters swam off, calling for Kishi.

"I'm coming, I'm coming," someone laughed, and then a mermaid with a straight black bob and a red-and-orange tail appeared at the surface. "Oh, hello!" she said in surprise. "I'm Kishi. I run the Sea Otter Summer Camp. Welcome, it's such an honour to meet you all. You've picked a brilliant day to visit us – it's our annual Sports Day!"

"Yay!" all the little otters cheered,

and Grace felt a burst of excitement as well. Sports Day was always one of her favourite events at school!

Layla didn't look as keen. "Oh no," she moaned. "I hate Sports Day, all that running around and getting hot."

"But it's a *Sea Otter* Sports Day!" Emily told her.

"Well, I might like that!" Layla conceded with a grin.

"We're going to have diving and swimming sprints and lots more!" Lola said, looking up at Grace, her big brown eyes shining with excitement.

"That sounds really fun," Grace told her, "but I'm very sorry, we can't stay.

We've got to look for a pearl. Has anyone seen one?"

The otters shook their heads.

"Oh, please stay!" Lola said, putting her paws together pleadingly. "It's definitely the best Sports Day in the whole entire ocean!"

Maya tapped on Emily's shoulder. "I'm going to catch the most sea urchins," she boasted.

"I'm sure you're going to be brilliant," Emily said, giving the otter a little hug.

"It's such a shame you can't stay. I could actually do with some help," Kishi admitted.

Grace glanced at the others. "Well, we

did promise to help all sea creatures . . ."
she reminded them.

Layla sighed dramatically, her eyes

twinkling with delight. "I mean, if you need us . . ."

Emily hugged Maya. "We'd love to stay!"

"Yay!" The little otters splashed and somersaulted happily.

Kishi clapped her hands in delight. "Let the Sports Day fun begin!"

Chapter Three

With a flick of her tail, Kishi dived
underwater. The otters followed her,
tumbling over each other as they
somersaulted through the water, down
into the kelp forest. The slimy seaweed
dragged against Grace's skin and tail
as she and her friends swam through
it, but the otters didn't seem to mind,
nimbly twisting and turning among the

green fronds. The water opened up into a clearing where there wasn't as much seaweed, and Kishi pointed up to the surface.

When they got up to the air, it was drizzling lightly. Drops of rain pattered on the sea around them as they bobbed at the water's surface.

"It always rains on Sports Day at our school too," Layla said. Luckily, none of them minded – after all, they were wet anyway!

"Welcome to Sports Day!" Kishi said. "It's always the highlight of our Sea Otter Summer Camp, but it's especially exciting today because we have four very

36

special guests: Princess Marina and the
Sea Keepers!"

The otters clapped their paws and
cheered. Layla gave a funny bow, Emily
looked embarrassed, Marina did a royal
wave and Grace grinned in excitement.

"I wonder if they'll have a sack race!"
Layla joked.

"Or an egg and spoon?" added Emily.

Kishi brought out a long, thin razor-
clam shell and blew into it, making a
piercing whistle. "Let the games begin!"
she announced as everyone whooped.
The otters piled their paws on top of each
other and then raised them up in the air
with a loud cheer.

"The first event will be the swimming sprints," Kishi declared. She swam over to the nearest kelp tree and pulled off a long piece of seaweed. "Sea Keepers, could I have your help? If you each take an end of this"– Kishi gave Grace one end and Emily the other – "you can be the finishing line! And Layla, you can blow the starting whistle."

"Now THAT is the kind of Sports Day activity I can do!" Layla giggled.

She swam over to the start, where the otters were already lined up. With a nod from Kishi, Layla blew into the clam shell, her face going red and cheeks puffing out as it let out a loud whistle.

The otters set off, racing towards Grace and Layla. Grace spotted Lola, appearing at the surface then disappearing underwater as she swam as fast as she could.

Grace and Emily held the seaweed ribbon tight as the otters sped towards it.

It was hard to tell which otter was which, but as one pulled into the lead Grace spotted a white speckle on her nose. It was Maya! She raced straight for the finishing line, breaking the seaweed.

"And the winner is Maya!" Kishi announced.

"Hooray!" everyone cheered. All the otters crowded round Maya to congratulate her. Kishi swam over and presented her with a golden shell, and Maya grinned from ear to ear.

"Next up, the Sea Urchin Dash!" Kishi said. "Whoever collects the most sea urchins in a minute wins!"

"Oooh!" the otters cried.

"Ready, steady, GO!" Kishi nodded at Layla and she blew the whistle again. Immediately all the otters disappeared, diving down  to the spiky urchins clustered on the sea bed. The water was much shallower in the clearing, so they didn't have to dive as far.

Grace, Marina and Emily held out a large piece of driftwood for the otters to put the urchins on.

"How do mermaids tell the time?"

Grace wondered out loud.

"Like this!" Marina said, gesturing towards where Kishi was submerging a shell underwater and counting the bubbles that floated up to the surface. Within seconds the first otters popped to the surface, each clutching a sea urchin. They put the spiny balls on the wood.

"That's one each for Rae, Adi, Maya and Lola," Emily said, keeping count.

The otters popped up again and again, piling urchins on the wood, then taking a deep breath and vanishing underwater again.

"Another for Rae!" Emily called out.

"One more for Lola," Marina added.

Grace watched anxiously as the otters raced up and down. "Lola's got four and so has Rae," she said. "It's going to be a close one!"

"Ten seconds left!" Kishi announced. As Lola dived down again, Rae popped up and put a fifth urchin on her pile.

"Time's up!" Kishi called out.

Layla blew the whistle.

Lola bobbed to the surface, a spiky sea urchin in her paw, but she was too late.

"Never mind," Grace whispered.

"It's OK. I'm definitely going to win the diving!" Lola said cheerfully. "Besides, I'm glad there are loads of sea urchins to eat at the feast later!"

"You eat them?" Emily eyed the urchins warily.

"Mmm!" Lola grinned and rubbed her tummy with a paw. "They're delicious!"

"Get ready for rock juggling!" Kishi called.

"Oh, I have to find my special rock, it's in my pocket," Lola said, patting her fur.

The girls laughed, thinking the cheeky otter was joking. But to their surprise, Lola reached towards her armpit and brought out a stone.

"You really do have a pocket!" Layla gasped.

"Yes!" Lola giggled. "Didn't you know? All sea otters have them."

"No way!" Grace exclaimed. Even Emily shook her head.

Lola showed them the fold of fur that made a little pocket under each armpit. "Most of us have a favourite stone that we carry with us. It's very useful. Watch!" She took out the rock and rolled over on to her back, still holding the sea urchin. She tapped the spiky shell with the stone until it cracked. Then she used her teeth to break the shell apart and eat the slimy treat inside.

"Hmm, I think I'll stick to chocolate," Layla said.

When Kishi gave the signal, the rock-juggling competition began. All the

45

otters floated on their backs and juggled rocks with their claws. They were all good at it, but Adi was the best – she kept three rocks in the air at the same time!

"I had no idea sea otters were so clever!" Grace exclaimed as Kishi announced that Adi was the winner and swam over to give him the golden shell. "Maybe we should ask them to solve the Mystic Clam's riddle?"

"Ooh, I love riddles!" Rae said.

"I bet I can help!" Lola agreed.

"Stuck between two plates deep down in the ground—" Marina started.

"Sea lion!" Adi called out in alarm.

Quick as a flash, the sea otters huddled together. Grace looked over to where a head was poking above the surface. It was smooth and dark grey, with long whiskers and small ears. Its eyes were glowing with a strange yellow light she'd seen before . . .

"Effluvia!" she gasped.

"Did someone call?" a voice asked.

A mermaid with midnight-blue hair and a deep purple tail appeared at the surface next to the sea lion. Effluvia's voice was beautiful, but there was a cruel smirk on her face.

"Oh, it's you again, two-legs," she said. "Don't you have anything better to do

47

than poking your noses into things that
don't concern you?"

"Nothing's more important than
stopping you!" Grace said bravely.

"Huh!" Effluvia scoffed. "I see you've
met my new pet, Leo." The sea lion
whispered in her ear. Effluvia's smirk

grew even wider and she patted him on the head.

Grace felt a horrible sinking feeling and a moment later her suspicions were confirmed.

Effluvia turned to face the girls, a nasty grin on her face. "Leo heard you say where the pearl is hidden! This time, you won't defeat me! I'm going to free my siren sisters and every pathetic, miserable little sea creature will tremble at our fins. Oh yes, I'm going to shake things up!

She took a deep breath and the girls instantly covered their ears with their hands.

"Don't listen to her!" Grace warned the

49

others. The sea otters put their little paws over their ears just in time, as Effluvia sang out a low note that gradually got higher and higher, echoing over the water. The waves began to shudder and crash as everything around them shook with the powerful force of Effluvia's magic.

"It's an earthquake!" Lola cried as a huge wave loomed over them.

Chapter Four

The giant wave crashed over them,
flinging salty spray up into the air. An
orange plastic buoy spun past Grace's
shoulder, and a piece of wood smacked
into Layla's side.

"Ouch!" she cried.

"Watch out! Here comes another one!"
Marina warned.

The wave smashed down next to

Grace. It was full of sand and stones
dredged up from the sea bed, so it was as
if the water was throwing rocks at her.

"Everyone go underwater, it'll be
calmer there!" Marina shouted above the
sound of the roaring waves.

"We can't leave the sea otters!" Emily cried.

"Yes, stay with your little friends!" Effluvia crowed as she bobbed in the violent waves. "They might be on their summer camp, but they don't look like very happy campers! While you look after those wet rats, I'll be searching for the pearl – and thanks to you I know just where to look! Fang and Leo, come along!" Giving a cruel laugh, she dived underwater, her fins coming down with a splash that sent another wave of water over the girls.

Grace wanted to chase after her, but then she glanced at the sea otters, who

were struggling in the thrashing water.
They had to stay and help them – it was
a Sea Keeper's job. She looked through
the stormy sea for Kishi, and caught sight
of her clinging to one of the kelp trees.

"What can we do, Kishi?" she yelled.

Kishi's reply was lost in the sound of
the crashing waves.

"What?" Grace asked again.

"GRAB HANDS!" Kishi shouted.
"HOLD THE KELP!"

Grace grabbed hold of the nearest
green stalk. The kelp was slippery, but
strong, swaying in the water like a tree
bending in the wind. She held on to it
tightly with one hand.

54

"Wrap the kelp around yourself like this," Rae told her, weaving the kelp with her paws. "Then we won't float away."

Grace wrapped the seaweed around her tail and tummy, then she reached for the otter's soft paw. Nearby, Emily, Layla and Marina were doing the same. One by one, the otters and mermaids gathered together, holding paws tightly, until they were all connected in a raft – and just in time, because the sea pelted them with another huge wave.

Layla swallowed a mouthful of water and Grace heard her gasp with shock. Layla shook her head to get her hair out of her eyes, but she didn't let go of Adi's

55

paw. The waves bounced them around,
sending them up high in the air then
quickly dropping them down. Grace
felt her tummy flip like she was on a
rollercoaster – but the kelp held fast.

"I'm frightened," Rae sobbed next
to her.

Grace didn't know what to say. Emily

and Layla were better at being reassuring
than she was. "Emily!" she called, but the
waves rolled and her words were lost in
the sound of the roaring water.

What would they say? Grace thought.
Emily would know a helpful fact and
Layla would probably sing to make
everyone happy. Actually, that wasn't

a bad idea . . . "Singing is good when you're frightened," Grace told the otter.

So, as the waves crashed around, Grace started singing a song from her favourite film. Emily and Layla heard the strains of the melody over the roaring storm and joined in. The sea otters started singing along too, once they'd figured out the words. Marina and Kishi added their beautiful mermaid voices and soon everyone was singing.

Between the waves, they could hear each other bravely singing. And gradually, the earthquake stopped and the water calmed.

"I think it's over," Layla said, peering

out through her wet hair.

The otters giggled nervously as they let go of each other's paws and ducked underwater to clean the sand and seaweed off their fur.

Grace untied the kelp from her waist and rinsed her arms and face in the sea. Emily and Layla swam over and the girls gave each other a big hug.

"That was so scary!" Emily said.

"Good idea about the singing," Layla told Grace.

"I learned it from you!" Grace said, grinning.

The clearing rang with relieved laughter for a second, until Kishi gave a

panicky shout. "Someone's missing!" she yelled.

The otters looked at each other in dismay as Kishi started counting them again.

"Where's Lola?" Rae squeaked.

"Lola? Lola?" the otters called.

Grace felt her tummy turn over like she was back on the wave rollercoaster. Where was Lola? Had she been injured? Or swept away by the waves?

"We have to find her!" Emily gasped.

"Everyone spread out and look for her!" Kishi said.

Grace dived underwater and pushed through the kelp forest. The sea bed was

churned up and the water was so full of sand that it was like swimming through grey mist.

Emily and Layla swam either side of her, and she could hear the other otters at the surface, searching and calling for their friend.

Grace strained her eyes. How were they ever going to find her?

"Lola!" she yelled. But there was no answer. Grace peered through the murky water, looking for a flash of brown otter fur.

The kelp forest was getting thicker and thicker. Grace was about to turn around and look somewhere else, when she saw

61

a dark shape wriggling in the seaweed up ahead. Was it an otter?

"Over there!" she yelled, kicking her fins to surge forward. Emily and Grace were right behind her as she swam deep into the underwater forest. The huge kelp trees were close together, the thick strands of seaweed intertwining. Moving through it was like pushing though a hedge made of slimy spaghetti.

As she got closer Grace could see that the shape was an otter – Lola! She was tangled up in the kelp. Grace could see her struggling, looking panicked.

"Lola, we're coming!" she yelled.

But as she pushed on, Emily gave a

cry from behind her. "I'm stuck!" she
shouted.

"Me too!" Layla called out.

Grace glanced back at them. "I have to rescue Lola first," she said. "We can breathe underwater, but she can't. I have to get her to the surface before she runs out of breath."

Emily nodded. "Go!"

"We'll be OK," Layla agreed.

Grace pushed on through the thick kelp.

Lola had spotted her and was waving frantically.

"I'll get you out—" Grace said, pushing through the thick forest. But the kelp twisted around her tail, pulling her back. She tried to untangle herself, but it just got tighter and tighter.

"Hold on, Lola, I'm coming," she called. She was so close she could almost touch the otter's paw, but it was no good. She was stuck too!

Grace looked at Lola helplessly as she yanked her tail again and again. The little sea otter desperately needed air. She had to get her free!

Chapter Five

Grace struggled against the slimy seaweed, but the more she twisted, the tighter the strands around her tail got, until they were cutting into her fins painfully. But she couldn't give up – she had to free Lola so the otter could go to the surface to breathe!

Lola looked so sad and defeated, nothing like how she'd been earlier,

diving and juggling rocks . . .

Suddenly, Grace had an idea. "Lola, do you still have a rock in your pocket?" she asked the otter.

Lola's eyes grew wide and she reached under her arm and pulled out a rock.

"Use it to cut through the kelp!" Grace urged her.

Lola nodded, then bent down and slashed at the seaweed tangle with the sharp edge of the rock.

"It's working!" Grace cheered as more and more kelp fell away. Suddenly, with a twist and a flick of her tail, Lola was free. "Go!" Grace cried.

Lola darted to the surface.

"She did it!" Grace yelled back to the others. "She's OK!"

After a few minutes, Lola appeared again, looking much happier. "Thank you so much!" she said. "I thought I was a goner." She dropped a rock into Grace's hands.

Grace used it to slice though the weeds wrapped around her tail. As soon as they fell away, she swam over to untangle the

others. Lola helped too, cutting through the kelp with her own rock.

When they were free, Emily and Layla gave Lola a big hug and then they all went up to the surface. Lola took a deep breath and then floated on her back happily. "Thank you so much, Sea Keepers," she grinned. "I never would have thought to use the rock without you."

"We're just glad you're OK," Emily said, stroking her soft fur.

"We'd better go and tell the others you're safe. Everyone is looking for you!" Layla told her.

They swam along the surface, over

the kelp forest and on to the clearing where the otter summer camp was. As they went, they could see lots of things that Effluvia's earthquake had destroyed. There was debris floating everywhere. A nearby boat was sinking, and another was upside down, a big crack along one side where it had been battered by the huge waves.

As they swam past the damage into the camp clearing, the water was shiny and rainbow-coloured, like the puddles they'd seen when they were kayaking in the harbour back at home.

"Ooh look, it's so pretty!" Lola said, swimming over to it.

"STOP!" yelled Marina.

Everyone stopped and looked over in surprise.

Marina swam over, looking concerned. "Lola, I'm so happy to see you!" she said, giving the otter a big hug. "But you can't touch that, it's engine oil! It must have come from the boats. The whole clearing is full of it."

"Oh no. I can't believe that's oil," Layla said.

"It's really bad for sea creatures, isn't it?" Emily whispered.

Marina nodded. "It can be deadly. It covers the feathers of seabirds so they can't fly, and if it gets on otter fur it stops

it from being waterproof. A sea otter's
fur is like a human wetsuit. It keeps them

warm and dry even when they're in the water, but oil lets the water in. If oil touches their fur, otters can die from the cold. Kishi's getting the others out of the water."

She nodded over to the shore, where Kishi was herding the otters. One by one they went up on to dry land. They gambolled on to the beach with little galloping hops, that reminded Grace of rabbits.

"Maya! Rae! Adi!" Lola called to her friends excitedly. On the beach the little otters were jumping up and down and waving.

"Come on!" Lola said, swimming

towards her friends. The others followed, but before she went, Grace glanced over at the rainbow-coloured water. It looked so beautiful, but it was deadly – just like Effluvia!

As Lola joined them on the beach, the otters crowded round her, making happy peeping sounds. They rolled on the sand and chased each other in and out of the water. Kishi sat on the beach too, splashing her red-and-orange tail in the shallow water and watching the otters.

It was a lovely scene, but Grace knew they couldn't stay. "Now that Lola's safe, we have to go after Effluvia," she said to the others in a low voice.

75

"She knows where the pearl is hidden," Emily said anxiously. "What if she's found it already?"

Marina shook her head. "We'd know if she had. She'd have made herself queen and released the sirens. She hasn't got it yet – but she might find it any second."

The girls called goodbye to the otters. "Good luck with the diving contest," Layla told Lola.

Kishi shook her head. "I'm afraid I'm going to have to cancel the diving contest. The water just isn't safe."

"Oh no!" Lola cried. All the otters' whiskers drooped sadly, but Lola looked the most miserable of all.

"Poor Lola. It's such a shame, she
worked so hard," Emily said.

"There's only one thing to do," Grace said determinedly. "We have to get that pearl and save Sports Day too!"

Chapter Six

"What are we waiting for, let's go!"
Grace said. The Sea Keepers and Marina
dived underwater together.

"So, Effluvia knows the first bit of the
riddle . . ." Emily said as they swam back
towards the crack. "But she doesn't know
the ending."

"**Stuck between two plates deep down in
the ground,**

Something must be broken for the pearl to be found," Marina recited.

"Well, we know the plates are where the crack is," Grace thought out loud.

"Ooh!" Layla gasped. "Maybe Effluvia did us a favour – maybe her earthquake broke something down there?"

Grace shrugged. "Only one way to find out!"

"Um, guys, don't be scared, but we're being followed," Marina laughed, pointing to a sleek shape racing after them – a cheeky little otter!

"Lola, what are you doing here?" Grace said in surprise.

"You should be with the others back on

the beach," Emily told her off gently.

But Lola shook her head. "You helped me," she said. "So I'm going to help you! I know these waters better than anyone. Besides, the sooner we find this pearl, the sooner I can win the diving contest!" She gave a cheeky grin.

The girls glanced at each other.

"It *would* be good to have someone who knows the area," Grace said practically.

"Exactly!" Lola said happily. "Come this way!"

They followed the little otter as she swam through the kelp forest and down to the crack. Grace shivered as the water grew darker and cooler.

The sand had settled back on to the sea bed, but the crack looked much wider than it had the last time they had seen it. There were broken boulders strewn about and smaller rocks scattered across the sea bed.

Everywhere they looked, creatures were repairing their homes after the storm.

"Just look at this mess!" a white crab said crossly, his bulging eyes darting from side to side. An enormous rock had crashed on to a bed of mussels and destroying the little crevice where the crab lived. He scuttled off sideways. But he wasn't the only angry animal about.

"Look!" Layla whispered.

It was Effluvia's sea lion, Leo! He swam over and started patrolling up and down the crack, guarding it from them. The girls ducked behind some kelp as the sea lion turned with a neat flick of his tail and sped back along the crevice.

"What are we going to do?" Layla whispered.

"Maybe we should wait until he has to go to the surface to breathe?" Grace suggested.

Marina shook her head. "Sea lions can hold their breath for twenty minutes," she told them. "That's even longer than sea otters."

"We can't wait that long," Grace said. "We have to find it before Effluvia does."

"I'll distract him!" Lola piped up.

Layla raised her hand in a question. "Um, don't sea lions eat otters?" she asked.

"Yes! It's too dangerous!" Emily said.

84

"I've got a better idea!" Grace said. "Why don't *we* distract it, while Lola uses her diving skills to go into the crack and look for the pearl?"

Lola didn't look convinced. "I'm really fast, you know. I really nearly won the swimming sprints earlier. Maya only won by a whisker!"

"Ah, but it will be great practice for your diving contest later!" Layla said cunningly.

"Good point!" Lola perked up, her whiskers twitching with excitement. "I'll do it!"

They quickly piled their hands one on top of each other, with Lola's paw on top.

85

"Go Sea Keepers!" Layla cheered.

Grace sped straight down towards Leo.
The huge sea lion turned swiftly as he
saw her coming. He was big and fast.
Now Grace understood how sea lions

could catch – and eat – the speedy sea
otters. But she couldn't think about that
right now.

"Over here!" she shouted.

"No, over here!" Emily yelled from the
left-hand side of the crack.

"Can't catch me!" Layla called as she
sped past on the right-hand side.

The sea lion looked from one girl to the
other with glowing yellow eyes. Then
Marina dived down behind him and Leo
sped towards her.

Grace carried on down to the sea bed.
As she got closer, she glanced over her
shoulder. Lola was hiding, waiting for
the right moment. When Grace nodded,

the brave little otter darted down to the crack. The sea lion twisted round, his eye caught by the flicker of movement, but Grace popped up in front of him.

"Looking for me?" she asked.

The sea lion turned his head, his tiny ears twitching as he looked from one Sea Keeper to the next.

"Come and get me!" Layla yelled. He gave a roar and headed off in her direction.

Grace kept a close eye on the crack. Lola was great at diving, but she couldn't hold her breath for ever. What if she got stuck again? Grace found that she was holding her own breath too, as she

waited for the cheeky otter to reappear.

Finally, she spotted Lola's little head poking out of the crack.

Grace raced in front of the sea lion. "Over here, you big meanie!" she yelled. This time she didn't dash away, but let Leo get so close that he was almost within biting distance of her fins before swimming off, giving Lola enough time to come out of the crack and go back to the surface to breathe.

When she thought she'd left it long enough, Grace swam as fast as she could into a thick patch of kelp. She waited among the green strands, her heart pounding. A moment later, the sea lion

burst into the kelp after her. "Now!"
Grace shouted. "Tie him up!" Marina,
Emily and Layla surrounded Leo and
quickly tangled him in the slimy kelp.

But the kelp wouldn't hold Leo for long – he was much too strong. He snapped his teeth viciously and thrashed his flippers, trying to break free.

"Quick! Let's go and find out what Lola saw," Grace said, leading the others up to the surface.

"There's a light glowing down there. I can take you to it," Lola told them proudly.

"Good work, Lola!" Layla praised her.

They all dived down again towards the crack, Lola leading the way.

The water was cold and dark, but in front of them was a dim golden light, right where Lola said it would be . . .

Arms outstretched, Grace swam towards the glow. But she stopped in horror as she was faced with the sight of needle-like teeth and googly eyes.

It wasn't the golden pearl – it was Effluvia's pet, Fang!

Chapter Seven

Grace stared at Fang in horror. The anglerfish had a light that hung over his sharp teeth, so he could lure small fish into his mouth. But right now, his mouth was open in surprise as he gazed back at her. Before Grace could even decide what to do, Fang was yelling. "Effluvia! Effluvia! The Sea Keepers are here!"

He turned tail and swam off as fast as

his fins could carry him, over to Effluvia.
The siren was scouring the crack between
the plates, searching for the pearl, but
she stopped when she heard Fang. Hands

on her hips, she
looked at the
girls with a cruel
expression on her
beautiful face.

"So, you got past
my sea lion, did
you?" she sneered,
flicking her dark-
blue hair. "Well,
you won't get past
me and Fang."

The fish puffed up his cheeks and tried to look tough.

Layla giggled.

Effluvia glanced down and elbowed Fang so hard he spat out a load of bubbles. "I might only know half the riddle, but that's enough! The pearl is somewhere in this crack and I won't let you Sea Keepers get anywhere near it!"

"We can't search with her here," Emily whispered.

"Come on," Grace said. "Let's work out a plan."

They hid behind a big rock.

"We have to get Effluvia away from here!" Layla told Marina.

"Maybe we can distract her like we did the sea lion," Emily thought out loud. "We could split into two teams . . ."

Grace's mind whirred as she tried to work out what to do. Effluvia and Fang were still searching the crack, and the sea lion was tangled in the kelp – for now. Leo thrashed against the seaweed as he tried desperately to return to his patrol duties.

"What are we going to d—" Marina stopped as Lola suddenly picked something up from the sea bed and swam up to the surface.

"Do you think she's found the pearl?" Layla asked hopefully.

They followed Lola up to the surface. When they got there, Lola was lying on her back with a mussel shell on her tummy.

"Sorry!" Lola said. "I know we need to find the pearl, but I'm *so* hungry and the mussels were right there! I was diving and then we started Sports Day and then there was the storm and I haven't had any lunch!" She bashed the mussel open on a rock, then she rolled on to her back and slurped down the squidgy mollusc inside greedily. "Yum! Do you want one? I can go and get more?" she offered.

The girls giggled. "No thanks, I prefer my seafood cooked," Layla joked.

But Emily was staring at the mussel shell like she'd been hypnotised by Effluvia. "Can I have that?" she asked.

"Sure!" Lola held out the two halves.

"What are you thinking?" Grace asked.

"*Stuck between two plates*," Emily said in a half-whisper, holding the two halves of the shell together.

"*Something must be broken for the pearl to be found*," Grace finished the riddle.

"I don't get it," Layla said.

"What if it's not in the crack at all," Emily explained. "Maybe the pearl is hidden inside a mussel shell!"

"We need to get those mussels," Layla said.

"Follow me! If collecting mussels was a Sports Day event, I'd definitely win!" Lola said. Taking a deep breath, she flipped over and dived down. Grace and the others swam after her.

There were so many mussels, all piled on top of each other and stuck on to the rocks like shells decorating a sandcastle. Lola showed them how to twist the mussels off, before shooting back up to the surface with her paws full of shells.

"I hope the sea otters enjoy these tasty snacks!" Layla said loudly as she spotted Fang lurking nearby.

"Oh yes, we'll need loads to feed all the otters at summer camp," Marina added with a wink.

They got back to the surface and swam over to the rock. Lola was already breaking another mussel open. "Delicious!" she said cheerfully. "No pearl inside though."

Grace and Layla started tapping their mussels on the rock, but Emily hesitated and Grace could tell she felt bad. "Don't worry, we really can give them to the sea otters," she said. "They won't go

100

to waste." Emily gave a nod, and then tapped her mussel on the rock. But there was no pearl inside.

"I'll have it!" Lola said, gobbling it up.

Grace bashed hers open, but there was no pearl in that one either. She put it on the rock and dived down for more. It wouldn't be long before Effluvia figured out what they were up to, so they had to be quick!

It took ages for her to pry the next mussel off the sea bed – she was nowhere near as fast as Lola.

"Let me help," said Lola, wrenching a few from the bottom with her claws and handing them out to the others. Grace

soon had three in each hand.

"I wish I had an armpit pocket!" Layla joked, trying not to drop any of the precious mussels. Their hands full, they all swam up to the surface and started cracking the shells against the rocks again.

"It's probably going to be in the last one we look in—" Layla said, then stopped talking as a yellow light spilled out of her mussel, illuminating her face with a beautiful golden gleam. It was the pearl!

"I've got it!" Layla yelled, then clamped her hand over her mouth.

They all looked around in alarm, but

Effluvia was far below them on the
sea bed.

"Quick, let's use the magic," Grace
said, swimming toward Layla. But before
she could get there, something rose out of

the water with a huge splash.

"It's Effluvia's sea lion!" cried Emily, warning her friends. "He's escaped from the kelp!"

Leo slapped Layla's hand with his flipper, flinging the pearl high into the air.

"The pearl!" Grace gasped. She watched in horror as it fell through the air and down into the foamy sea.

She dived, focusing on the tiny golden dot plunging through the water.

But she wasn't the only one. Leo was after it too, using his powerful flippers to race towards it. His mouth was open, showing teeth as sharp as a real lion's.

Grace kicked her fins and reached out, grabbing the precious pearl. Then she swam over to Lola. "Quick! Give me your rock and put this in your pocket," she whispered, thrusting the pearl into the otter's paws as Lola swiftly passed her the rock. And just

 105

in time, because the sea lion was right behind her.

"You want it, go get it!" Grace yelled, throwing Lola's stone down on to the mussel bed. She desperately hoped her plan would work!

Chapter Eight

With a roar, the sea lion dived after Lola's rock, thinking it was the pearl.

"Phew!" Grace sighed in relief, once the coast was clear.

Lola brought the shimmering pearl out of her pocket.

"Thank you," Grace said, stroking the otter's soft fur. "If there was an event for being brave you'd win that too!"

She took the pearl and held it out to her friends. "Now let's save your Sports Day!"

Emily and Layla put their hands on the pearl and Grace said, "I wish for the damage from Effluvia's earthquake to be repaired!"

Colourful swirls of mermaid magic bubbled in the water around the pearl, and when it disappeared, the light in the pearl had gone too. They'd done it!

"I'm sorry I lost your favourite stone," Grace said to Lola. "But you can keep the pearl instead if you want?"

Lola grinned as she tucked it away in her pocket. "I can find another rock,

but this is special. I'll keep it to always remember you."

A moment later, Effluvia appeared with Fang and the sea lion.

"He got it!" gloated Effluvia. "My sea lion found the pearl."

"Are you sure about that?" Grace asked her, arching one eyebrow.

The sea lion swam over to Effluvia and dropped Lola's rock into the siren's hand.

Effluvia let out a furious shriek. She flung the rock, hitting Leo on the head. He blinked, and the yellow glow disappeared from his eyes.

Layla nudged the others. "He's not hypnotised any more!" she whispered.

Now, the sea
lion was staring
at Effluvia,
looking very
cross. He swam
towards her, his
tiny ears back and a
fierce look on his face.

Effluvia clutched Fang like a teddy
bear, looking frightened.

"Get lost, you horrible siren! I never
want to see you again!" the sea lion
barked angrily. He chased Effluvia and
Fang away.

"Effluvia's going so fast she could
win the Sports Day swimming sprints,"

joked Layla, as they watched the siren disappear from view.

They gathered up the mussels they'd cracked earlier and swam back to the summer camp. Back in the clearing, the water was clean and calm – except for the splashing coming from the sea otters having fun!

"Adi, Rae, I've saved the day!" Lola called as she swam over to join her friends. The Sea Keepers handed out the mussels and the otters tucked in happily.

"Thank you so much," Kishi cried as she saw them. "The camp looks perfect again! The water is clear."

"Does this mean you can have the

111

diving competition?" Grace asked.

"Oh yes, please!" the otters cried. They crowded round Kishi, all talking at once.

"We've been practising—"

"I'm the best—"

"OK, OK!" Kishi laughed. "Let's go over to the deeper water."

Lola swam over to the girls, her brown eyes shining with excitement.

"Good luck, Lola!" Emily said.

"You can do it!" Layla cheered.

"Whether you win or not, your diving is brilliant," Grace said. "Without your help, we wouldn't have found the pearl."

"Effluvia might have got it!" Layla said with a shudder.

"Why don't you come underwater with me?" Kishi suggested. "It's the best place to watch."

They dived down into the water and waited. "This is a better view than the royal box," Marina said, laughing.

Kishi blew into the razor-clam shell, and the first otter dived down.

The girls clapped as Rae swam through the water, her cheeks puffed out. She barely got halfway to the sea bed before she turned back and swam up for air.

One by one, the otters had a go.

"Lola is definitely the best," Layla said.

"It's her turn next!" Emily said, crossing her fingers anxiously.

Grace felt a bit worried too. She took part in lots of swimming competitions and she knew how tough it could be. Lola had already had so many adventures today. Would she have any energy left for the dive? Grace crossed her fingers too, and so did Layla.

Then Lola dived into the water. She swam down past the girls easily, and gave them a cheeky wave. She swam deeper and deeper, all the way to the bottom where she scooped up a rock, then shot back up to the surface in a cloud of bubbles.

Grace, Layla and Emily whooped happily as they followed their otter friend

up to the surface.

Lola and her
friends were
already
celebrating as
Kishi held out
a golden shell.
"The winner of
the diving competition

is Lola!" Kishi said as the otters clapped
their paws and the Sea Keepers cheered.

"Would you like to stay for the feast?"
Kishi said, pointing at the sea urchins
they'd collected earlier.

"Oh yay, I'm starving!" Lola cheered,
waving her new rock in the air.

"You just ate all those mussels!" Layla laughed.

"Swimming makes you hungry!" Lola told her.

"But you're a sea otter – you're always swimming!" Emily giggled.

"That's probably why I'm always hungry!" Lola said with a grin.

Grace looked at her friends. It would be great to hang out with the adorable sea otters a bit longer, but they needed to go home. She couldn't stop thinking about the oil they'd seen while they were kayaking. They'd cleaned up the spills here, but back home they couldn't use magic to get rid of the oil.

116

"We should get back," she said. "We've got another oil spill to clear up."

Layla and Emily nodded seriously. Even though they didn't have their mermaid tails back home, they were always Sea Keepers – and they'd promised to protect the seas.

"Marina, can you send us home now?" Emily asked.

"Lola can have my share of the urchins!" Layla joked.

Marina nodded. "Thank you for your help, Sea Keepers. I'll call you the next time the Mystic Clam remembers where a pearl is hidden."

The girls hugged the otters goodbye, then Marina sang the song to send them home, her beautiful voice surrounding them with mermaid magic:

**"Send the Sea Keepers back to land,
Until we need them to lend a hand."**

A moment later they were back behind the beach huts, standing on the sand.

118

Grace wriggled her toes happily. She loved being a mermaid, but it was always nice to have her legs back. She did a cartwheel as they went along the beach, looking out for the rainbow puddles on the water.

"I think it's coming from that boat!" Emily said, pointing to a small motor boat.

"It's called *Starfish*," Grace said, squinting to read the writing on the boat's side. *Starfish* was surrounded by the colourful oil. It didn't look so beautiful now they knew what it was!

"Maybe Pranav will know who the boat belongs to," Layla said, looking at

where the instructor was locking the door of the boat shed. No time ever passed while they were away, so he had no idea they'd just been on an exciting mermaid adventure!

"Pranav, do you know who owns that boat?" Grace asked, pointing to Starfish.

Pranav nodded. "Yeah, that's my boat. Why?"

"Oh!" Grace said in surprise. "Um, I think it's got an oil leak," she told him.

"Oh yeah, it's been like that for a few days. I need to get it fixed," Pranav said casually.

Grace glanced at her friends. She really liked Pranav and she was sure he

wouldn't want to hurt anyone. "It's just that oil is really bad for sea creatures," she said.

"Did you know if it gets on sea otter fur they can die?" Emily said.

"Even a little oil leak is dangerous," Layla added.

"Really?" Pranav said, looking ashamed. "I didn't know that. I'll fix it tomorrow morning. I promise."

"That would be amazing!" Emily said in relief.

"Thanks for telling me, girls," Pranav said. "I'll put a poster up asking all the other boat owners to check their engines as well, OK?"

"That would be great!" Grace said.

"The sea otters say thank you," Emily told him.

"Well, they would if they could talk," Layla said. "Which they can, but humans just can't understand them.

Mermaids can understand, though—"

Grace put her hand over her friend's mouth. "I think you've had too much sun, Layla! Thank you, Pranav, see you at our next lesson."

As the girls walked up the hill, they heard the chimes of an ice cream van.

"Ooh, ice cream!" Layla said.

"Now that really is a feast!" said Emily.

"Lola was right," Grace said as she linked arms with her friends and they ran up to the ice cream van. "Swimming really does make you hungry!"

The End

Join Emily, Grace and Layla
for another adventure in …

The Rainbow Seahorse

Emily was sitting on her bed, surrounded by a mountain of clothes.

"Whoa!" Mum said as she came in, wiping her hands on her apron. "Has there been a hurricane in here?"

Emily giggled. "I'm trying to decide what to wear for our fancy-dress party tonight!"

Mum grinned. "I can't believe it's been a whole year since we opened the Mermaid Café."

Emily looked out of her window. Over the tops of the houses she could see the deep blue of the sea, twinkling in the morning sunshine, and seagulls swooping through the cloudless sky. She could hear the happy hum of people talking and chatting in the café downstairs, along with the chink of cups and the hiss of the coffee machine. She'd been so worried when they first moved to Sandcombe, and now she never wanted to live anywhere else!

Read **The Rainbow Seahorse** to find out what happens next!

How to be a real-life

Would you like to be a Sea Keeper just like Emily, Grace and Layla? Here are a few ideas for how you can help protect our oceans.

1. Try to use less water
Using too much water is wasteful. Turn off the tap when you brush your teeth and take shorter showers.

2. Use fewer plastic products
Plastic ends up in the ocean and can cause problems for marine wildlife. Instead of using plastic bottles, refill a metal bottle. Carry a tote bag when out shopping, and use non-disposable food containers and cutlery.

Sea Keeper

3. Help at a beach clean-up
Keeping the shore clear of litter means less litter is swept into the sea. Next time you're at the beach or a lake, try and pick up all the litter you can see.

4. Reduce your energy consumption
Turn off lights when you aren't using a room. Walk or cycle instead of driving. Take the stairs instead of the lift. Using less energy helps reduce the effects of climate change.

5. Avoid products that harm marine life
Do not buy items made from endangered species. If you eat seafood, make sure it comes from sustainable sources.

Dive into a mermaid adventure!

The Mermaid's Dolphin
Coral Ripley

The Sea Unicorn
Coral Ripley

Coral Reef Rescue
Coral Ripley

Sea Turtle School
Coral Ripley

Penguin Island
Coral Ripley

Sea Otter
Summer Camp
Coral Ripley

The Rainbow Seahorse
Coral Ripley

Coming Soon

Whale Song Wedding
Coral Ripley

The Missing Manatee
Coral Ripley

Starfish Sleepover
Coral Ripley

Seal Cub Surprise
Coral Ripley